This book belongs to:

_____

For Paul, Ellen and Luca

This paperback edition first published in 2013 by Andersen Press Ltd.
First published in Great Britain in 1996 by Andersen Press Ltd.,
20 Vauxhall Bridge Road, London SW1V 2SA.
Published in Australia by Random House Australia Pty.,
Level 3, 100 Pacific Highway, North Sydney, NSW 2060.
Copyright © David McKee, 1996.
The rights of David McKee to be identified as the author and illustrator of this work
have been asserted by him in accordance with the Copyright, Designs and Patents Act, 1988.
All rights reserved. Colour separated in Switzerland by Photolitho AG, Zürich.
Printed and bound in Singapore by Tien Wah Press.

10   9   8   7   6   5   4   3   2   1

British Library Cataloguing in Publication Data available.

ISBN 978 1 84270 331 1

CHARLOTTE'S PIGGY BANK

David McKee

Andersen Press

One day, when they were out together, Aunt Jane
bought Charlotte a present.

"Thank you, Aunt Jane," said Charlotte, as she
unwrapped it. "It's . . . it's a pig," she said in surprise.

"It's a piggy bank – a money box," said Aunt Jane.

"And this will start your savings." She put some
money into the pig.

"Thank you, Aunt Jane," said Charlotte.

"Silly present," said Charlotte as she went indoors and she shook the pig to try to get the money out.

"Don't do that," said the pig. "It hurts."

"Oh! A magic pig," said Charlotte.

"Yes," said the pig. "And if you save enough you get a wish."

"Save enough?" said Charlotte. "I thought they gave wishes away. How much must I save?"

"When you've saved enough," said the pig, "you'll hear a 'DING!'"

"I could be saving for ever," said Charlotte.

"Life can be very hard," said the pig.

"I'm saving for a wish," said Charlotte, when she was given her pocket money.

"I expect wishes are expensive," said Dad, and he gave an extra coin.

Later, Charlotte put the money in the pig. It didn't 'DING!' and the pig didn't speak again.

"I'm saving for a wish," said Charlotte as she
helped her mum.

"That's nice, dear," said Mum and she found some
coins for Charlotte's savings.

There still wasn't a 'DING!' from the pig.

Charlotte took Mr Jack's dog for walks. She liked
to help the neighbours.

"This is for being so kind," said Jack as he gave
Charlotte some money. Still the pig didn't 'DING!'

Mrs Adams wrote letters and Charlotte posted them.
"Here's a little something for being so helpful," said
Mrs Adams. The little something didn't 'DING!' the
pig either.

When Mr Grant washed his car, Charlotte helped him. They sang duets as they worked.

"That's for being so sweet," said Mr Grant, and he gave her some coins. The coins made a nice sound as they fell into the pig, but it wasn't a 'DING!'

Charlotte made a stall in the street
and sold the toys that she didn't
want any more. "You're nearly full,"
said Charlotte as she put the money
in the pig. The pig said nothing.

When Charlotte visited Aunt Jane again, Aunt Jane said, "This is for the pig," and gave Charlotte a big silver coin.

"Thank you, Aunt Jane," said Charlotte. "I'm saving for a wish."

Aunt Jane's coin did it. 'DING!' went the pig.
"Hurrah, I get my wish!" shouted Charlotte.
"Yes, and I'm glad you wished that," said the pig.
"Wished what?" said Charlotte.
"You said you wished I was a flying pig," said the pig.
"I never said that," gasped Charlotte.
"You never said what?" asked the pig.

"I wish you were a flying pig,"
said Charlotte.
  "That's it," said the pig
and there was a flash. There stood
the pig, only bigger and with wings.
  "That's not fair, you tricked me,"
said Charlotte. "Where's my wish?
Where's my money?"

"Life can be very hard," said the pig as he flew out of the window.
"Come back," shouted Charlotte.
"Perhaps," said the pig.